SNUGGLE, SNIGGLE, AND SOMETIMES SNICKLE

Snuggle, Sniggle, and Sometimes Snickle by Stephen Spivey
Cover and Illustration by Adam Hembrough.

Published by BooBoo Bär Publishing

© 2017 Stephen John Spivey

www.thesnugglebook.com

ISBN 978-0-692-07938-6

For my son, John Michael, and my wife, D. D., who fill my days with joy. I am blessed beyond compare. Numbers 6:24-26

- Stephen

For my wife, Kenda, who is my encourager, best friend, and the love of my life. Proverbs 18:22

- Adam

Sometimes when I wake up early,
my mommy and daddy are on each side of me.

It is kind of like a snuggle sandwich.

I will snuggle
with my mommy...

and then I will snuggle
with my daddy.

Snuggling is warm, cozy, and feels like love.

I can snuggle
when I am happy.

... or when
I am sad.

I like to snuggle with my pets, too.

My dog likes to snuggle...

and my cat likes to snuggle.

My fish and I
have a special snuggle.

Did you know there are different kinds of snuggling?

The classic snuggle, the sniggle, and the snickle!

A sniggle is a snuggle with a giggle added in!

We can family sniggle when we are watching our favorite movie.

Then there are the
super fun times when we snickle.

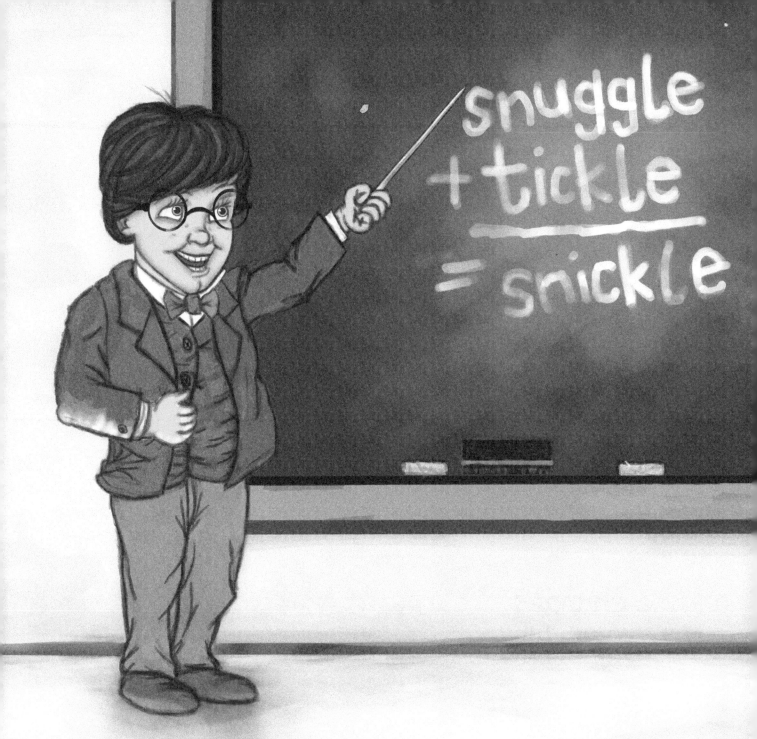

A snickle is a snuggle with a tickle added in!

My daddy likes to be sneaky sometimes when we are snuggling..

and he changes it to a snickle.

Often times, I imagine that I am a wildlife biologist and get to snuggle with my favorite animals.

I snuggle with a gorilla.

Now I know how my cat feels!

Sniggle with a hyena.

It is true – hyenas like to laugh!

Snickle with a zebra.

AAAAAAAAAAAAAAAAAAA

AAAHHH!

Well, maybe not with a zebra.

A busy day of bringing snuggles to others
can be quite exhausting.

At the end of the day,
after I have brushed my teeth...

and put on my pajamas, I need something
that is warm, cozy, and feels like love.

I need a snuggle.

And I dream about the next day when I can...

snuggle, sniggle, and sometimes snickle.

CPSIA information can be obtained
at www.ICGtesting.com
Printed in the USA
LVHW070958241118
598005LV00016BA/147/P

9 780692 079386